Weekly Reader Books presents

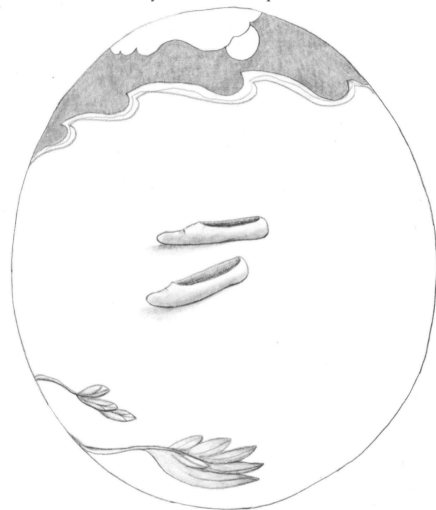

The Dancing Man

story and pictures by RUTH BORNSTEIN

A Clarion Book • The Seabury Press • New York

Other Clarion Books by Ruth Bornstein

Jim
The Dream of the Little Elephant
Little Gorilla

This book is a presentation of
Weekly Reader Books.

Weekly Reader Books offers
book clubs for children from
preschool through junior high school.
All quality hardcover books are selected by
a distinguished Weekly Reader Selection Board.

For further information write to:
Weekly Reader Books
1250 Fairwood Ave.
Columbus, Ohio 43216

The Seabury Press, 815 Second Avenue, New York, New York 10017

Copyright © 1978 by Ruth Bornstein

Printed in the United States of America

Library of Congress Cataloging in Publication Data
Bornstein, Ruth.   The dancing man.
"A Clarion book."
SUMMARY: Wearing his pair of special silver shoes,
young Joseph sets out to dance with the world.
[1. Dancing—Fiction] I. Title.
PZ7.B64848Dan   [E]   77-29124   ISBN 0-8164-3214-7

For Jonah
For Janice
For Jacob

Once, in a poor village by the Baltic Sea,
there lived an orphan boy named Joseph.
When he was still very small, Joseph knew that life
in the village was dreary and hard.
No one laughed. No one danced.
But Joseph saw that all around him the world danced.

Fire danced in the hearth. Trees swayed with the wind.
Clouds danced in the sky.
Even the sun and the moon moved across the heavens.
When his work was done, Joseph ran to the shore
and felt in his bones how the waves danced in the sea.
And Joseph longed to move, to sway, to dance with the world.
He dreamed that, one day, he would dance down the road
from village to village, even as far as the southernmost sea.
But he told no one. No one would understand.

One evening, when the wind blew and silver clouds flew
over the water, an old man appeared on the shore.
He wore a long red coat, a tall green hat, and on his feet
a pair of silver shoes.

The old man put out a foot.
One slow step, one quick step, a glide, a dip . . .
the old man was dancing the waves!
Joseph's heart beat fast. He drew near.

The old man swept off his hat and bowed.
"I'm the Dancing Man," he said,
"and I have a gift for you."

He danced down the shore. Joseph followed.

A sharp gust of wind blew Joseph around.

When he turned back, the old man was gone.

But there, in the sand, lay the silver shoes.

And Joseph knew they were meant for him.

Joseph hid the shoes in an old barn near the sea.
"Now I know that one day I will have the courage,"
he said aloud. "I will dance down the road
even as far as the southernmost sea. When the shoes fit,
I must be ready."

Every day Joseph watched the world around him.
Every day he felt in his bones all the ways
the world danced. The years flew by.
And one day, the shoes fit.

Joseph came into the village. Slowly he began to dance.
A child followed. Then another.
Slowly the people turned to one another and smiled.
Slowly they joined hands.
And Joseph danced with the people in his silver shoes.

Joseph knew he was ready. He said goodbye to the people.
It was time to leave.

Joseph put out a foot.

One slow step. One quick step. One slow step . . .

Suddenly he turned, he leaped, he pranced, he danced,

down the road in his silver shoes.

He danced for his supper at an inn and slept under
the stars, his shoes on the earth beside him.
He made his way through one town, then another.
With the coins he earned, he bought a long blue coat
and a tall yellow hat.

An old woman gave him a flower.

And Joseph danced with the flower.

The road led Joseph through dark forests and far valleys,
through crowded places and silent places.
And in all these places, down all the paths,
Joseph felt in his bones all the ways the world danced.

Once he came upon a weary pedlar with his mule and his cart.
The mule kicked up his heels. Joseph kicked up his heels.
A rat scuttled out from under the cart. Joseph scuttled.
The pedlar laughed until his cheeks grew red,
and for a moment he forgot his cares.

The pedlar shared his bread with Joseph and asked him to stay.
It was good there with the friendly pedlar but Joseph said,
"I must follow the road to the next village."
And he danced down the road in his silver shoes.

Once, when winter lay bitter along the road,
Joseph came to a great house where a young girl lay,
ill and in pain.
Joseph danced the snow melting and the first small bird
of spring. He danced the sun and the small bird singing
to the sun. And in her pain, the young girl smiled.

The people of the house gave Joseph gold coins and asked him
to stay. It was good and warm there in the great house,
but Joseph said, "I must follow the road to the next village."
And he danced down the road in his silver shoes.

Once, when summer lay heavy along the road,
Joseph stopped to rest and watch the frogs in a stream.
That night, in the next village, he saw the children
peek from behind their doors.
Joseph began to jump and hop
in such a funny way that the children laughed and knew
he danced a frog. The children forgot their fear of the night

for they too danced and were frogs and streams
and stars and moons.
The children asked Joseph to stay.
And oh, it was good and sweet there with the children.
But Joseph said, "I must follow the road all through
the land, even as far as the southernmost sea."
And he danced down the road in his silver shoes.

And once on a tired day . . . after many summers and winters, springs and autumns . . . Joseph saw smoke curling from a sturdy farmhouse. Beside the house he saw bountiful fields. He saw an old farmer harvesting the fields.

Joseph stood still in the road.
Suddenly the road seemed too long, the journey too lonely.
"The farmer is blessed with a good life," thought Joseph.
"He lives in a snug house. He works the land.
He reaps a fine harvest."

Before he knew it, Joseph put out a foot.

He began to dance.

He danced the sowing of the seeds and the green crops growing.

He danced the fruits ripening.

He danced the fine harvest.

The farmer leaned on his pitchfork and watched.

Then his old face shone with understanding.

Joseph took his hand, and together Joseph and the farmer
danced in the fields.

Suddenly Joseph laughed. He laughed for joy.
"Why, I too am blessed. I too reap a fine harvest,
a harvest of dances. And I share my fine harvest
with everyone I meet."

Just then a soft wind came down the road.
A leaf twirled slowly in the wind. Slowly Joseph twirled.
The leaf twirled faster. Joseph twirled faster.
Before the farmer could ask him to stay, Joseph called,
'Goodbye, I must follow the road to the next village."
And Joseph twirled faster, faster, down the road
in his silver shoes.

On his way through the years, down all the paths,
fires still danced in hearths, trees danced with the wind.
And Joseph still felt in his bones
how well and good the world danced.
But then, at last, after many summers and winters,
springs and autumns, Joseph's bones grew old with time.

Joseph climbed slowly up the next hill.
He stood on the hill and smiled.
He smiled as he remembered the boy he had been,
standing on the shore of the Baltic Sea.
He smiled because he had done what he had dreamed of doing
long ago. He had danced down the road, all through the land,
even as far as the southernmost sea.

Joseph looked down at his feet.
Through the dust the silver shoes still shone.
Joseph bent and brushed the dust away.
There was one more thing he must do.

Joseph stepped down to the water.

A small figure stood alone on the shore.

Joseph's heart beat fast. He began to dance.

One slow step, one quick step, a glide, a dip . . .

The boy drew near.
Joseph knew the words to say.

He swept off his hat and bowed.

"I'm the Dancing Man," he said,

"and I have a gift for you."